DOVER
CHILDREN'S THRIFT CLASSICS

The Elephant's Child and Other Just So Stories

RUDYARD KIPLING

Illustrated by Thea Kliros

DOVER PUBLICATIONS, INC.
New York

DOVER CHILDREN'S THRIFT CLASSICS
EDITOR: PHILIP SMITH

Bibliographical Note

The Elephant's Child and Other Just So Stories is a new selection of six stories from *Just So Stories for Little Children*, first published by Doubleday, Page & Company, New York, 1902. The stories are printed here unabridged; however, the author's original illustrations (and illustration captions) have been replaced with new illustrations by Thea Kliros (with the exception of the numbered figures in the last story, which are Kipling's). A new introductory Note has also been specially prepared for this edition.

Library of Congress Cataloging-in-Publication Data

Kipling, Rudyard, 1865–1936.
    [Just so stories for little children. Selections]
    The Elephant's child and other Just so stories / Rudyard Kipling ; illustrated by Thea Kliros.
        p.   cm. — (Dover children's thrift classics)
    "A new selection of six stories from Just so stories for little children, first published by Doubleday, Page & Company, New York, 1902"—T.p. verso.
    Contents: The Elephant's child — How the Camel got his hump — The sing-song of Old Man Kangaroo — The beginning of the Armadilloes — How the first letter was written — How the alphabet was made.
    ISBN 0-486-27821-2 (pbk.)
    1. Children's stories, English. [1. Animals—Fiction. 2. Short stories.] I. Kliros, Thea, ill. II. Title. III. Series.
PZ7.K632E1   1993
[Fic]—dc20   93–2460
                                                    CIP
                                                       AC

Manufactured in the United States of America
Dover Publications, Inc., 31 East 2nd Street, Mineola, N.Y. 11501

Note

Rudyard Kipling's playful command of the English language and his flair for storytelling both in prose and verse forms have made him a favorite of readers young and old since his works first began appearing in the 1880s. Born in India to British parents in 1865, Kipling grew up in an atmosphere whose exoticism and natural features were to form the framework of his literary endeavors.

Just So Stories, from which the six stories in this volume are taken [the other six are available in *How the Leopard Got His Spots and Other Just So Stories* (0-486-27297-4), also in the Dover Children's Thrift Classics series], represents, along with the *Jungle Books*, *Kim* and *Captains Courageous*, one of Kipling's enduring contributions to the literature of childhood. Refined versions of stories composed orally for the amusement of his children, the tales in *Just So Stories* have long been popular for their imaginative recountings of natural phenomena (a motif found in folk tales) as well as for the sparkle and humor of their wordplay, and have continued to entertain generations born long after their author's death in 1936.

Contents

List of Illustrations

The Elephant's Child

IN THE HIGH and Far-Off Times the Elephant, O Best Beloved, had no trunk. He had only a blackish, bulgy nose, as big as a boot, that he could wriggle about from side to side; but he couldn't pick up things with it. But there was one Elephant—a new Elephant—an Elephant's Child—who was full of 'satiable curtiosity, and that means he asked ever so many questions. *And* he lived in Africa, and he filled all Africa with his 'satiable curtiosities. He asked his tall aunt, the Ostrich, why her tail-feathers grew just so, and his tall aunt the Ostrich spanked him with her hard, hard claw. He asked his tall uncle, the Giraffe, what made his skin spotty, and his tall uncle, the Giraffe, spanked him with his hard, hard hoof. And still he was full of 'satiable curtiosity! He asked his broad aunt, the Hippopotamus, why her eyes were red, and his broad aunt, the Hippopotamus, spanked him with her broad, broad hoof; and he asked his hairy uncle, the Baboon, why melons tasted just so, and his hairy uncle, the Baboon, spanked him with his hairy, hairy paw. And *still* he was full of 'satiable curtiosity! He asked questions about everything that he saw, or heard, or felt, or smelt, or touched, and all his uncles and his aunts spanked him. And still he was full of 'satiable curtiosity!

One fine morning in the middle of the Precession of the Equinoxes this 'satiable Elephant's Child asked a new fine question that he had never asked before. He asked, 'What does the Crocodile have for dinner?' Then everybody said, 'Hush!' in a loud and dretful tone, and they spanked him immediately and directly, without stopping, for a long time.

By and by, when that was finished, he came upon Kolokolo Bird sitting in the middle of a wait-a-bit thorn-bush, and he said, 'My father has spanked me, and my mother has spanked me; all my aunts and uncles have spanked me for my 'satiable curtiosity; and *still* I want to know what the Crocodile has for dinner!'

Then Kolokolo Bird said, with a mournful cry, 'Go to the banks of the great grey-green, greasy Limpopo River, all set about with fever-trees, and find out.'

That very next morning, when there was

nothing left of the Equinoxes, because the Precession had preceded according to precedent, this 'satiable Elephant's Child took a hundred pounds of bananas (the little short red kind), and a hundred pounds of sugarcane (the long purple kind), and seventeen melons (the greeny-crackly kind), and said to all his dear families, 'Good-bye. I am going to the great grey-green, greasy Limpopo River, all set about with fever-trees, to find out what the Crocodile has for dinner.' And they all spanked him once more for luck, though he asked them most politely to stop.

Then he went away, a little warm, but not at all astonished, eating melons, and throwing the rind about, because he could not pick it up.

He went from Graham's Town to Kimberley, and from Kimberley to Khama's Country, and from Khama's Country he went east by north, eating melons all the time, till at last he came to the banks of the great grey-green, greasy Limpopo River, all set about with fever-trees, precisely as Kolokolo Bird had said.

Now you must know and understand, O Best Beloved, that till that very week, and day, and hour, and minute, this 'satiable Elephant's Child had never seen a Crocodile, and did not know what one was like. It was all his 'satiable curtiosity.

The first thing that he found was a Bi-Coloured-Python-Rock-Snake curled round a rock.

' 'Scuse me,' said the Elephant's Child most politely, 'but have you seen such a thing as a Crocodile in these promiscuous parts?'

'*Have* I seen a Crocodile?' said the Bi-Coloured-Python-Rock-Snake, in a voice of dretful scorn. 'What will you ask me next?'

' 'Scuse me,' said the Elephant's Child, 'but could you kindly tell me what he has for dinner?'

Then the Bi-Coloured-Python-Rock-Snake uncoiled himself very quickly from the rock, and spanked the Elephant's Child with his scalesome, flailsome tail.

'That is odd,' said the Elephant's Child, 'because my father and my mother, and my uncle and my aunt, not to mention my other aunt, the Hippopotamus, and my other uncle, the Baboon, have all spanked me for my 'satiable curtiosity—and I suppose this is the same thing.'

So he said good-bye very politely to the Bi-Coloured-Python-Rock-Snake, and helped to coil him up on the rock again, and went on, a little warm, but not at all astonished, eating melons, and throwing the rind about, because he could not pick it up, till he trod on what he thought was a log of wood at the very edge of the great grey-green, greasy Limpopo River, all set about with fever-trees.

But it was really the Crocodile, O Best Beloved, and the Crocodile winked one eye — like this!

' 'Scuse me,' said the Elephant's Child most politely, 'but do you happen to have seen a Crocodile in these promiscuous parts?'

Then the Crocodile winked the other eye, and lifted half his tail out of the mud; and the Elephant's Child stepped back most politely, because he did not wish to be spanked again.

'Come hither, Little One,' said the Crocodile. 'Why do you ask such things?'

' 'Scuse me,' said the Elephant's Child most politely, 'but my father has spanked me, my mother has spanked me, not to mention my tall aunt, the Ostrich, and my tall uncle, the Giraffe, who can kick ever so hard, as well as my broad aunt, the Hippopotamus, and my hairy uncle, the Baboon, *and* including the Bi-Coloured-Python-Rock-Snake, with the scale-some, flailsome tail, just up the bank, who spanks harder than any of them; and *so*, if it's quite all the same to you, I don't want to be spanked any more.'

'Come hither, Little One,' said the Crocodile, 'for I am the Crocodile,' and he wept crocodile-tears to show it was quite true.

Then the Elephant's Child grew all breathless, and panted, and kneeled down on the bank and said, 'You are the very person I have been looking for all these long days. Will you please tell me what you have for dinner?'

'Come hither, Little One,' said the Crocodile, 'and I'll whisper.'

Then the Elephant's Child put his head down close to the Crocodile's musky, tusky mouth, and the Crocodile caught him by his little nose, which up to that very week, day, hour, and minute, had been no bigger than a boot, though much more useful.

'I think,' said the Crocodile—and he said it between his teeth, like this—'I think to-day I will begin with Elephant's Child!'

At this, O Best Beloved, the Elephant's Child was much annoyed, and he said, speaking through his nose, like this, 'Led go! You are hurtig be!'

Then the Bi-Coloured-Python-Rock-Snake scuffled down from the bank and said, 'My young friend, if you do not now, immediately and instantly, pull as hard as ever you can, it is my opinion that your acquaintance in the large-pattern leather ulster' (and by this he meant the Crocodile) 'will jerk you into yonder limpid stream before you can say Jack Robinson.'

This is the way Bi-Coloured-Python-Rock-Snakes always talk.

Then the Elephant's Child sat back on his little haunches, and pulled, and pulled, and pulled, and his nose began to stretch. And the Crocodile floundered into the water, making it all creamy with great sweeps of his tail, and *he* pulled, and pulled, and pulled.

And the Elephant's Child's nose kept on stretching; and the Elephant's Child spread all his little four legs and pulled, and pulled, and pulled, and his nose kept on stretching; and the Crocodile threshed his tail like an oar, and *he* pulled, and pulled, and pulled, and at each pull the Elephant's Child's nose grew longer and longer—and it hurt him hijjus!

Then the Elephant's Child felt his legs slipping, and he said through his nose, which was now nearly five feet long, 'This is too butch for be!'

Then the Bi-Coloured-Python-Rock-Snake came down from the bank, and knotted himself in a double-clove-hitch round the Elephant's Child's hind-legs, and said, 'Rash and inexperienced traveller, we will now seriously devote ourselves to a little high tension,

At each pull the Elephant's Child's nose grew
longer and longer.

because if we do not, it is my impression that yonder self-propelling man-of-war with the armour-plated upper deck' (and by this, O Best Beloved, he meant the Crocodile) 'will permanently vitiate your future career.'

That is the way all Bi-Coloured-Python-Rock-Snakes always talk.

So he pulled, and the Elephant's Child pulled, and the Crocodile pulled; but the Elephant's Child and the Bi-Coloured-Python-Rock-Snake pulled hardest; and at last the Crocodile let go of the Elephant's Child's nose with a plop that you could hear all up and down the Limpopo.

Then the Elephant's Child sat down most hard and sudden; but first he was careful to say 'Thank you' to the Bi-Coloured-Python-Rock-Snake; and next he was kind to his poor pulled nose, and wrapped it all up in cool banana leaves, and hung it in the great grey-green, greasy Limpopo to cool.

'What are you doing that for?' said the Bi-Coloured-Python-Rock-Snake.

' 'Scuse me,' said the Elephant's Child, 'but my nose is badly out of shape, and I am waiting for it to shrink.'

'Then you will have to wait a long time,' said the Bi-Coloured-Python-Rock-Snake.

'Some people do not know what is good for them.'

The Elephant's Child sat there for three days waiting for his nose to shrink. But it never grew any shorter, and, besides, it made him squint. For, O Best Beloved, you will see and understand that the Crocodile had pulled it out into a really truly trunk same as all Elephants have to-day.

At the end of the third day a fly came and stung him on the shoulder, and before he knew what he was doing he lifted up his trunk and hit that fly dead with the end of it.

' 'Vantage number one!' said the Bi-Coloured-Python-Rock-Snake. 'You couldn't have done that with a mere-smear nose. Try and eat a little now.'

Before he thought what he was doing the Elephant's Child put out his trunk and plucked a large bundle of grass, dusted it clean against his fore-legs, and stuffed it into his own mouth.

' 'Vantage number two!' said the Bi-Coloured-Python-Rock-Snake. 'You couldn't have done that with a mere-smear nose. Don't you think the sun is very hot here?'

'It is,' said the Elephant's Child, and before he thought what he was doing he schlooped up a schloop of mud from the banks of the great grey-green, greasy Limpopo, and slapped it on his head, where it made a cool schloopy-sloshy mud-cap all trickly behind his ears.

' 'Vantage number three!' said the Bi-Coloured-Python-Rock-Snake. 'You couldn't have done that with a mere-smear nose. Now how do you feel about being spanked again?'

' 'Scuse me,' said the Elephant's Child, 'but I should not like it at all.'

'How would you like to spank somebody?' said the Bi-Coloured-Python-Rock-Snake.

'I should like it very much indeed,' said the Elephant's Child.

'Well,' said the Bi-Coloured-Python-Rock-Snake, 'you will find that new nose of yours very useful to spank people with.'

'Thank you,' said the Elephant's Child, 'I'll remember that; and now I think I'll go home to all my dear families and try.'

So the Elephant's Child went home across Africa frisking and whisking his trunk. When he wanted fruit to eat he pulled fruit down from a tree, instead of waiting for it to fall as he used to do. When he wanted grass he plucked grass up from the ground, instead of going on his knees as he used to do. When the flies bit him he broke off the branch of a tree and used it as a fly-whisk; and he made him-

self a new, cool, slushy-squshy mud-cap
whenever the sun was hot. When he felt
lonely walking through Africa he sang to himself down his trunk, and the noise was louder
than several brass bands. He went especially
out of his way to find a broad Hippopotamus
(she was no relation of his), and he spanked
her very hard, to make sure that the Bi-
Coloured-Python-Rock-Snake had spoken the
truth about his new trunk. The rest of the
time he picked up the melon rinds that he had
dropped on his way to the Limpopo—for he
was a Tidy Pachyderm.

One dark evening he came back to all his
dear families, and he coiled up his trunk and
said, 'How do you do?' They were very glad to
see him, and immediately said, 'Come here
and be spanked for your 'satiable curtiosity.'

'Pooh,' said the Elephant's Child. 'I don't
think you peoples know anything about
spanking; but *I* do, and I'll show you.'

Then he uncurled his trunk and knocked
two of his dear brothers head over heels.

'O Bananas!' said they, 'where did you learn
that trick, and what have you done to your
nose?'

'I got a new one from the Crocodile on the
banks of the great grey-green, greasy Limpopo
River,' said the Elephant's Child. 'I asked him

what he had for dinner, and he gave me this to keep.'

'It looks very ugly,' said his hairy uncle, the Baboon.

'It does,' said the Elephant's Child. 'But it's very useful,' and he picked up his hairy uncle, the Baboon, by one hairy leg, and hove him into a hornet's nest.

Then that bad Elephant's Child spanked all his dear families for a long time, till they were very warm and greatly astonished. He pulled out his tall Ostrich aunt's tail-feathers; and he caught his tall uncle, the Giraffe, by the hind-leg, and dragged him through a thorn-bush; and he shouted at his broad aunt, the Hippo-potamus, and blew bubbles into her ear when she was sleeping in the water after meals; but he never let any one touch Kolokolo Bird.

At last things grew so exciting that his dear families went off one by one in a hurry to the banks of the great grey-green, greasy Limpopo River, all set about with fever-trees, to borrow new noses from the Crocodile. When they came back nobody spanked anybody any more; and ever since that day, O Best Beloved, all the Elephants you will ever see, besides all those that you won't, have trunks precisely like the trunk of the 'satiable Elephant's Child.

I KEEP six honest serving-men
    (They taught me all I knew);
Their names are What and Why and When
    And How and Where and Who.
I send them over land and sea,
    I send them east and west;
But after they have worked for me,
    I give them all a rest.

I let them rest from nine till five,
    For I am busy then,
As well as breakfast, lunch, and tea,
    For they are hungry men:
But different folk have different views;
    I know a person small—
She keeps ten million serving-men,
    Who get no rest at all!
She sends 'em abroad on her own affairs,
    From the second she opens her eyes—
One million Hows, two million Wheres,
    And seven million Whys!

How the Camel Got His Hump

Now THIS IS the next tale, and it tells how the Camel got his big hump.

In the beginning of years, when the world was so new-and-all, and the Animals were just beginning to work for Man, there was a Camel, and he lived in the middle of a Howling Desert because he did not want to work; and besides, he was a Howler himself. So he ate sticks and thorns and tamarisks and milkweed and prickles, most 'scruciating idle; and when anybody spoke to him he said 'Humph!' Just 'Humph!' and no more.

Presently the Horse came to him on Monday morning, with a saddle on his back and a bit in his mouth, and said, 'Camel, O Camel, come out and trot like the rest of us.'

'Humph!' said the Camel; and the Horse went away and told the Man.

Presently the Dog came to him, with a stick in his mouth, and said, 'Camel, O Camel,

15

come and fetch and carry like the rest of us.'

'Humph!' said the Camel; and the Dog went away and told the Man.

Presently the Ox came to him, with the yoke on his neck, and said, 'Camel, O Camel, come and plough like the rest of us.'

'Humph!' said the Camel; and the Ox went away and told the Man.

At the end of the day the Man called the Horse and the Dog and the Ox together, and said, 'Three, O Three, I'm very sorry for you (with the world so new-and-all); but that Humph-thing in the Desert can't work, or he would have been here by now, so I am going to leave him alone, and you must work double-time to make up for it.'

That made the Three very angry (with the world so new-and-all), and they held a pala-ver, and an *indaba*, and a *punchayet*, and a pow-wow on the edge of the Desert; and the Camel came chewing milkweed *most* 'scruci-ating idle, and laughed at them. Then he said 'Humph!' and went away again.

Presently there came along the Djinn in charge of All Deserts, rolling in a cloud of dust (Djinns always travel that way because it is Magic), and he stopped to palaver and pow-wow with the Three.

'Djinn of All Deserts,' said the Horse, '*is* it right for any one to be idle, with the world so new-and-all?'

'Certainly not,' said the Djinn.

'Well,' said the Horse, 'there's a thing in the middle of your Howling Desert (and he's a Howler himself) with a long neck and long legs, and he hasn't done a stroke of work since Monday morning. He won't trot.'

'Whew!' said the Djinn, whistling, 'that's my Camel, for all the gold in Arabia! What does he say about it?'

'He says "Humph!" ' said the Dog; 'and he won't fetch and carry.'

'Does he say anything else?'

'Only "Humph!"; and he won't plough,' said the Ox.

'Very good,' said the Djinn. 'I'll humph him if you will kindly wait a minute.'

The Djinn rolled himself up in his dust-cloak, and took a bearing across the desert, and found the Camel most 'scruciatingly idle, looking at his own reflection in a pool of water.

'My long and bubbling friend,' said the Djinn, 'what's this I hear of your doing no work, with the world so new-and-all?'

'Humph!' said the Camel.

The Djinn sat down, with his chin in his

'Humph!' said the Camel.

hand, and began to think a Great Magic, while the Camel looked at his own reflection in the pool of water.

'You've given the Three extra work ever since Monday morning, all on account of your 'scruciating idleness,' said the Djinn; and he went on thinking Magics, with his chin in his hand.

'Humph!' said the Camel.

'I shouldn't say that again if I were you,' said the Djinn; 'you might say it once too often. Bubbles, I want you to work.'

And the Camel said 'Humph!' again; but no sooner had he said it than he saw his back, that he was so proud of, puffing up and puffing up into a great big lolloping humph.

'Do you see that?' said the Djinn. 'That's your very own humph that you've brought upon your very own self by not working. To-day is Thursday, and you've done no work since Monday, when the work began. Now you are going to work.'

'How can I,' said the Camel, 'with this humph on my back?'

'That's made a-purpose,' said the Djinn, 'all because you missed those three days. You will be able to work now for three days without eating, because you can live on your humph; and don't you ever say I never did anything for you. Come out of the Desert and go to the Three, and behave. Humph yourself!'

And the Camel humphed himself, humph and all, and went away to join the Three. And from that day to this the Camel always wears a humph (we call it 'hump' now, not to hurt his feelings); but he has never yet caught up with the three days that he missed at the beginning of the world, and he has never yet learned how to behave.

THE Camel's hump is an ugly lump
   Which well you may see at the Zoo;
But uglier yet is the hump we get
   From having too little to do.

Kiddies and grown-ups too-oo-oo,
If we haven't enough to do-oo-oo,
     We get the hump—
     Cameelious hump—
The hump that is black and blue!

We climb out of bed with a frouzly head
   And a snarly-yarly voice.
We shiver and scowl and we grunt and we growl
   At our bath and our boots and our toys;

And there ought to be a corner for me
(And I know there is one for you)
     When we get the hump—
     Cameelious hump—
The hump that is black and blue!

The cure for this ill is not to sit still,
   Or frowst with a book by the fire;
But to take a large hoe and a shovel also,
   And dig till you gently perspire;

And then you will find that the sun and the wind,
And the Djinn of the Garden too,
     Have lifted the hump—
     The horrible hump—
The hump that is black and blue!

I get it as well as you-oo-oo—
If I haven't enough to do-oo-oo!
    We all get hump—
    Cameelious hump—
Kiddies and grown-ups too!

The Sing-Song of Old Man Kangaroo

NOT ALWAYS WAS the Kangaroo as now we do behold him, but a Different Animal with four short legs. He was grey and he was woolly, and his pride was inordinate: he danced on an outcrop in the middle of Australia, and he went to the Little God Nqa.

He went to Nqa at six before breakfast, saying, 'Make me different from all other animals by five this afternoon.'

Up jumped Nqa from his seat on the sand-flat and shouted, 'Go away!'

He was grey and he was woolly, and his pride was inordinate: he danced on a rock-ledge in the middle of Australia, and he went to the Middle God Nquing.

He went to Nquing at eight after breakfast, saying, 'Make me different from all other animals; make me, also, wonderfully popular by five this afternoon.'

Up jumped Nquing from his burrow in the spinifex and shouted, 'Go away!'

He was grey and he was woolly, and his pride was inordinate: he danced on a sand-bank in the middle of Australia, and he went to the Big God Nqong.

He went to Nqong at ten before dinner-time, saying, 'Make me different from all other animals; make me popular and wonderfully run after by five this afternoon.'

Up jumped Nqong from his bath in the salt-pan and shouted, 'Yes, I will!'

Nqong called Dingo—Yellow-Dog Dingo—always hungry, dusty in the sunshine, and showed him Kangaroo. Nqong said, 'Dingo! Wake up, Dingo! Do you see that gentleman dancing on an ashpit? He wants to be popular and very truly run after. Dingo, make him so!'

Up jumped Dingo—Yellow-Dog Dingo—and said, 'What, *that* cat-rabbit?'

Off ran Dingo—Yellow-Dog Dingo—always hungry, grinning like a coal-scuttle,—ran after Kangaroo.

Off went the proud Kangaroo on his four little legs like a bunny.

This, O Beloved of mine, ends the first part of the tale!

He ran through the desert; he ran through the mountains; he ran through the salt-pans;

he ran through the reed-beds; he ran through the blue gums; he ran through the spinifex; he ran till his front legs ached.

He had to!

Still ran Dingo—Yellow-Dog Dingo—always hungry, grinning like a rat-trap, never getting nearer, never getting farther,—ran after Kangaroo.

He had to!

Still ran Kangaroo—Old Man Kangaroo. He ran through the ti-trees; he ran through the mulga; he ran through the long grass; he ran through the short grass; he ran through the Tropics of Capricorn and Cancer; he ran till his hind legs ached.

He had to!

Still ran Dingo—Yellow-Dog Dingo—hungrier and hungrier, grinning like a horse-collar, never getting nearer, never getting farther; and they came to the Wollgong River.

Now, there wasn't any bridge, and there wasn't any ferry-boat, and Kangaroo didn't know how to get over; so he stood on his legs and hopped.

He had to!

He hopped through the Flinders; he hopped through the Cinders; he hopped through the deserts in the middle of Australia. He hopped like a Kangaroo.

First he hopped one yard; then he hopped three yards; then he hopped five yards; his legs growing stronger; his legs growing longer. He hadn't any time for rest or refreshment, and he wanted them very much.

Still ran Dingo—Yellow-Dog Dingo—very much bewildered, very much hungry, and wondering what in the world or out of it made Old Man Kangaroo hop.

For he hopped like a cricket; like a pea in a saucepan; or a new rubber ball on a nursery floor.

He had to!

He tucked up his front legs; he hopped on his hind legs; he stuck out his tail for a balance-weight behind him; and he hopped through the Darling Downs.

He had to!

Still ran Dingo—Tired-Dog Dingo—hungrier and hungrier, very much bewildered, and wondering when in the world or out of it would Old Man Kangaroo stop.

Then came Nqong from his bath in the salt-pans, and said, 'It's five o'clock.'

Down sat Dingo—Poor-Dog Dingo—always hungry, dusty in the sunshine; hung out his tongue and howled.

Down sat Kangaroo—Old Man Kangaroo—stuck out his tail like a milking-stool behind

He tucked up his front legs; he hopped on his hind
legs.

him, and said, 'Thank goodness *that's* finished!'

Then said Nqong, who is always a gentleman, 'Why aren't you grateful to Yellow-Dog Dingo? Why don't you thank him for all he has done for you?'

Then said Kangaroo—Tired Old Kangaroo—'He's chased me out of the homes of my childhood; he's chased me out of my regular mealtimes; he's altered my shape so I'll never get it back; and he's played Old Scratch with my legs.'

Then said Nqong, 'Perhaps I'm mistaken, but didn't you ask me to make you different from all other animals, as well as to make you very truly sought after? And now it is five o'clock.'

'Yes,' said Kangaroo. 'I wish that I hadn't. I thought you would do it by charms and incantations, but this is a practical joke.'

'Joke!' said Nqong, from his bath in the blue gums. 'Say that again and I'll whistle up Dingo and run your hind legs off.'

'No,' said the Kangaroo. 'I must apologise. Legs are legs, and you needn't alter 'em so far as I am concerned. I only meant to explain to Your Lordliness that I've had nothing to eat since morning, and I'm very empty indeed.'

'Yes,' said Dingo—Yellow-Dog Dingo,—'I am

just in the same situation. I've made him different from all other animals; but what may I have for my tea?"

Then said Nqong from his bath in the salt-pan, 'Come and ask me about it to-morrow, because I'm going to wash.'

So they were left in the middle of Australia, Old Man Kangaroo and Yellow-Dog Dingo, and each said, 'That's *your* fault.'

THIS is the mouth-filling song
Of the race that was run by a Boomer,
Run in a single burst—only event of its kind—
Started by Big God Nqong from Warrigaborriga-
    rooma,
Old Man Kangaroo first: Yellow-Dog Dingo behind.

Kangaroo bounded away,
His back-legs working like pistons—
Bounded from morning till dark,
Twenty-five feet to a bound.
Yellow-Dog Dingo lay
Like a yellow cloud in the distance—
Much too busy to bark.
My! but they covered the ground!

Nobody knows where they went,
Or followed the track that they flew in,
For that Continent
Hadn't been given a name.
They ran thirty degrees,
From Torres Straits to the Leeuwin
(Look at the Atlas, please),
And they ran back as they came.

S'posing you could trot
From Adelaide to the Pacific,
For an afternoon's run—
Half what these gentlemen did—
You would feel rather hot,
But your legs would develop terrific—
Yes, my importunate son,
You'd be a Marvellous Kid!

The Beginning of the Armadilloes

THIS, O BEST BELOVED, is another story of the High and Far-Off Times. In the very middle of those times was a Stickly-Prickly Hedgehog, and he lived on the banks of the turbid Amazon, eating shelly snails and things. And he had a friend, a Slow-Solid Tortoise, who lived on the banks of the turbid Amazon, eating green lettuces and things. And so *that* was all right, Best Beloved. Do you see?

But also, and at the same time, in those High and Far-Off Times, there was a Painted Jaguar, and he lived on the banks of the turbid Amazon too; and he ate everything that he could catch. When he could not catch deer or monkeys he would eat frogs and beetles; and when he could not catch frogs and beetles he went to his Mother Jaguar, and she told him how to eat hedgehogs and tortoises.

She said to him ever so many times,

graciously waving her tail, 'My son, when you find a Hedgehog you must drop him into the water and then he will uncoil, and when you catch a Tortoise you must scoop him out of his shell with your paw.' And so that was all right, Best Beloved.

One beautiful night on the banks of the turbid Amazon, Painted Jaguar found Stickly-Prickly Hedgehog and Slow-Solid Tortoise sitting under the trunk of a fallen tree. They could not run away, and so Stickly-Prickly curled himself up into a ball, because he was a Hedgehog, and Slow-Solid Tortoise drew in his head and feet into his shell as far as they would go, because he was a Tortoise; and so *that* was all right, Best Beloved. Do you see?

'Now attend to me,' said Painted Jaguar, 'because this is very important. My mother said that when I meet a Hedgehog I am to drop him into the water and then he will uncoil, and when I meet a Tortoise I am to scoop him out of his shell with my paw. Now which of you is Hedgehog and which is Tortoise? because, to save my spots, I can't tell.'

'Are you sure of what your Mummy told you?' said Stickly-Prickly Hedgehog. 'Are you quite sure? Perhaps she said that when you uncoil a Tortoise you must shell him out of the water with a scoop, and when you paw

One beautiful night Painted Jaguar found Stickly-
Prickly Hedgehog and Slow-Solid Tortoise sitting
under the trunk of a fallen tree.

a Hedgehog you must drop him on the shell.'

'Are you sure of what your Mummy told you?' said Slow-and-Solid Tortoise. 'Are you quite sure? Perhaps she said that when you water a Hedgehog you must drop him into your paw, and when you meet a Tortoise you must shell him till he uncoils.'

'I don't think it was at all like that,' said Painted Jaguar, but he felt a little puzzled; 'but, please, say it again more distinctly.'

'When you scoop water with your paw you uncoil it with a Hedgehog,' said Stickly-Prickly. 'Remember that, because it's important.'

'*But,*' said the Tortoise, 'when you paw your meat you drop it into a Tortoise with a scoop. Why can't you understand?'

'You are making my spots ache,' said Painted Jaguar; 'and besides, I didn't want your advice at all. I only wanted to know which of you is Hedgehog and which is Tortoise.'

'I shan't tell you,' said Stickly-Prickly. 'But you can scoop me out of my shell if you like.'

'Aha!' said Painted Jaguar. 'Now I know you're Tortoise. You thought I wouldn't! Now I will.' Painted Jaguar darted out his paddy-paw just as Stickly-Prickly curled himself up, and

of course Jaguar's paddy-paw was just filled
with prickles. Worse than that, he knocked
Stickly-Prickly away and away into the woods
and the bushes, where it was too dark to find
him. Then he put his paddy-paw into his
mouth, and of course the prickles hurt him
worse than ever. As soon as he could speak he
said, 'Now I know he isn't Tortoise at all.
But'—and then he scratched his head with his
un-prickly paw—'how do I know that this
other is Tortoise?'

'But I *am* Tortoise,' said Slow-and-Solid.
'Your mother was quite right. She said that
you were to scoop me out of my shell with
your paw. Begin.'

'You didn't say she said that a minute ago,'
said Painted Jaguar, sucking the prickles out
of his paddy-paw. 'You said she said something quite different.'

'Well, suppose you say that I said that she
said something quite different, I don't see that
it makes any difference; because if she said
what you said I said she said, it's just the
same as if I said what she said she said. On
the other hand, if you think she said that you
were to uncoil me with a scoop, instead of
pawing me into drops with a shell, I can't help
that, can I?'

'But you said you wanted to be scooped out of your shell with my paw,' said Painted Jaguar.

'If you'll think again you'll find that I didn't say anything of the kind. I said that your mother said that you were to scoop me out of my shell,' said Slow-and-Solid.

'What will happen if I do?' said the Jaguar most sniffily and most cautious.

'I don't know, because I've never been scooped out of my shell before; but I tell you truly, if you want to see me swim away you've only got to drop me into the water.'

'I don't believe it,' said Painted Jaguar. 'You've mixed up all the things my mother told me to do with the things that you asked me whether I was sure that she didn't say, till I don't know whether I'm on my head or my painted tail; and now you come and tell me something I *can* understand, and it makes me more mixy than before. My mother told me that I was to drop one of you two into the water, and as you seem so anxious to be dropped I think you don't want to be dropped. So jump into the turbid Amazon and be quick about it.'

'I warn you that your Mummy won't be pleased. Don't tell her I didn't tell you,' said Slow-Solid.

'If you say another word about what my mother said—' the Jaguar answered, but he had not finished the sentence before Slow-and-Solid quietly dived into the turbid Amazon, swam under water for a long way, and came out on the bank where Stickly-Prickly was waiting for him.

'That was a very narrow escape,' said Stickly-Prickly. 'I don't like Painted Jaguar. What did you tell him that you were?'

'I told him truthfully that I was a truthful Tortoise, but he wouldn't believe it, and he made me jump into the river to see if I was, and I was, and he is surprised. Now he's gone to tell his Mummy. Listen to him!'

They could hear Painted Jaguar roaring up and down among the trees and the bushes by the side of the turbid Amazon, till his Mummy came.

'Son, son!' said his mother ever so many times, graciously waving her tail, 'what have you been doing that you shouldn't have done?'

'I tried to scoop something that said it wanted to be scooped out of its shell with my paw, and my paw is full of per-ickles,' said Painted Jaguar.

'Son, son!' said his mother ever so many times, graciously waving her tail, 'by the prickles in your paddy-paw I see that that must have been a Hedgehog. You should have dropped him into the water.'

'I did that to the other thing; and he said he was a Tortoise, and I didn't believe him, and it was quite true, and he has dived under the turbid Amazon, and he won't come up again, and I haven't anything at all to eat, and I think we had better find lodgings somewhere else. They are too clever on the turbid Amazon for poor me!'

'Son, son!' said his mother ever so many times, graciously waving her tail, 'now attend to me and remember what I say. A Hedgehog curls himself up into a ball and his prickles stick out every which way at once. By this you may know the Hedgehog.'

'I don't like this old lady one little bit,' said Stickly-Prickly, under the shadow of a large leaf. 'I wonder what else she knows?'

'A Tortoise can't curl himself up,' Mother Jaguar went on, ever so many times, graciously waving her tail. 'He only draws his head and legs into his shell. By this you may know the Tortoise.'

'I don't like this old lady at all—at all,' said Slow-and-Solid Tortoise. 'Even Painted Jaguar can't forget those directions. It's a great pity that you can't swim, Stickly-Prickly.'

'Don't talk to me,' said Stickly-Prickly. 'Just

think how much better it would be if you could curl up. This *is* a mess! Listen to Painted Jaguar.'

Painted Jaguar was sitting on the banks of the turbid Amazon sucking prickles out of his paws and saying to himself—

> 'Can't curl, but can swim—
> Slow-Solid, that's him!
> Curls up, but can't swim—
> Stickly-Prickly, that's him!'

'He'll never forget that this month of Sundays,' said Stickly-Prickly. 'Hold up my chin, Slow-and-Solid. I'm going to try to learn to swim. It may be useful.'

'Excellent!' said Slow-and-Solid; and he held up Stickly-Prickly's chin, while Stickly-Prickly kicked in the waters of the turbid Amazon.

'You'll make a fine swimmer yet,' said Slow-and-Solid. 'Now, if you can unlace my back-plates a little, I'll see what I can do towards curling up. It may be useful.'

Stickly-Prickly helped to unlace Tortoise's back-plates, so that by twisting and straining Slow-and-Solid actually managed to curl up a tiddy wee bit.

'Excellent!' said Stickly-Prickly; 'but I

shouldn't do any more just now. It's making you black in the face. Kindly lead me into the water once again and I'll practise that side-stroke which you say is so easy.' And so Stickly-Prickly practised, and Slow-Solid swam alongside.

'Excellent!' said Slow-and-Solid. 'A little more practice will make you a regular whale. Now, if I may trouble you to unlace my back and front plates two holes more, I'll try that fascinating bend that you say is so easy. Won't Painted Jaguar be surprised!'

'Excellent!' said Stickly-Prickly, all wet from the turbid Amazon. 'I declare, I shouldn't know you from one of my own family. Two holes, I think, you said? A little more expression, please, and don't grunt quite so much, or Painted Jaguar may hear us. When you've finished, I want to try that long dive which you say is so easy. Won't Painted Jaguar be surprised!'

And so Stickly-Prickly dived, and Slow-and-Solid dived alongside.

'Excellent!' said Slow-and-Solid. 'A leetle more attention to holding your breath and you will be able to keep house at the bottom of the turbid Amazon. Now I'll try that exercise of wrapping my hind legs round my ears which you say is so peculiarly comfortable. Won't Painted Jaguar be surprised!'

'Excellent!' said Stickly-Prickly. 'But it's straining your back-plates a little. They are all overlapping now, instead of lying side by side.'

'Oh, that's the result of exercise,' said Slow-and-Solid. 'I've noticed that your prickles seem to be melting into one another, and that you're growing to look rather more like a pine-cone, and less like a chestnut-burr, than you used to.'

'Am I?' said Stickly-Prickly. 'That comes from my soaking in the water. Oh, won't Painted Jaguar be surprised!'

They went on with their exercises, each helping the other, till morning came; and when the sun was high they rested and dried themselves. Then they saw that they were both of them quite different from what they had been.

'Stickly-Prickly,' said Tortoise after break-fast, 'I am not what I was yesterday; but I think that I may yet amuse Painted Jaguar.'

'That was the very thing I was thinking just now,' said Stickly-Prickly. 'I think scales are a tremendous improvement on prickles—to say nothing of being able to swim. Oh, *won't* Painted Jaguar be surprised! Let's go and find him.'

By and by they found Painted Jaguar, still nursing his paddy-paw that had been hurt the night before. He was so astonished that he fell three times backward over his own painted tail without stopping.

'Good morning!' said Stickly-Prickly. 'And how is your dear gracious Mummy this morning?'

'She is quite well, thank you,' said Pointed Jaguar; 'but you must forgive me if I do not at this precise moment recall your name.'

'That's unkind of you,' said Stickly-Prickly, 'seeing that this time yesterday you tried to scoop me out of my shell with your paw.'

'But you hadn't any shell. It was all prickles,' said Painted Jaguar. 'I know it was. Just look at my paw!'

'You told me to drop into the turbid Amazon and be drowned,' said Slow-Solid. 'Why are you so rude and forgetful to-day?'

'Don't you remember what your mother told you?' said Stickly-Prickly,—

'Can't curl, but can swim—
Stickly-Prickly, that's him!
Curls up, but can't swim—
Slow-Solid, that's him!'

Then they both curled themselves up and

rolled round and round Painted Jaguar till his eyes turned truly cart-wheels in his head.

Then he went to fetch his mother.

'Mother,' he said, 'there are two new animals in the woods to-day, and the one that you said couldn't swim, swims, and the one that you said couldn't curl up, curls; and they've gone shares in their prickles, I think, because both of them are scaly all over, instead of one being smooth and the other very prickly; and, besides that, they are rolling round and round in circles, and I don't feel comfy.'

'Son, son!' said Mother Jaguar ever so many times, graciously waving her tail, 'a Hedgehog is a Hedgehog, and can't be anything but a Hedgehog; and a Tortoise is a Tortoise, and can never be anything else.'

'But it isn't a Hedgehog, and it isn't a Tortoise. It's a little bit of both, and I don't know its proper name.'

'Nonsense!' said Mother Jaguar. 'Everything has its proper name. I should call it "Armadillo" till I found out the real one. And I should leave it alone.'

So Painted Jaguar did as he was told, especially about leaving them alone; but the curious thing is that from that day to this, O Best Beloved, no one on the banks of the turbid

Amazon has ever called Stickly-Prickly and Slow-Solid anything except Armadillo. There are Hedgehogs and Tortoises in other places, of course (there are some in my garden); but the real old and clever kind, with their scales lying lippety-lappety one over the other, like pine-cone scales, that lived on the banks of the turbid Amazon in the High and Far-Off Days, are always called Armadilloes, because they were so clever.

So *that's* all right, Best Beloved. Do you see?

I'vᴇ never sailed the Amazon,
　I've never reached Brazil;
But the *Don* and *Magdalena*,
　They can go there when they will!

　　　　Yes, weekly from Southampton,
　　　　Great steamers, white and gold,
　　　　Go rolling down to Rio
　　　　(Roll down—roll down to Rio!)
　　　　And I'd like to roll to Rio
　　　　Some day before I'm old!

I've never seen a Jaguar,
　Nor yet an Armadill—
O dilloing in his armour,
　And I s'pose I never will,

　　　　Unless I go to Rio
　　　　These wonders to behold—
　　　　Roll down—roll down to Rio—
　　　　Roll really down to Rio!
　　　　Oh, I'd love to roll to Rio
　　　　Some day before I'm old!

How the First Letter Was Written

ONCE UPON a most early time was a Neolithic man. He was not a Jute or an Angle, or even a Dravidian, which he might well have been, Best Beloved, but never mind why. He was a Primitive, and he lived cavily in a Cave, and he wore very few clothes, and he couldn't read and he couldn't write and he didn't want to, and except when he was hungry he was quite happy. His name was Tegumai Bopsulai, and that means, 'Man-who-does-not-put-his-foot-forward-in-a-hurry'; but we, O Best Beloved, will call him Tegumai, for short. And his wife's name was Teshumai Tewindrow, and that means, 'Lady-who-asks-a-very-many-questions'; but we, O Best Beloved, will call her Teshumai, for short. And his little girl-daughter's name was Taffimai Metallumai, and that means, 'Small-person-without-any-manners-who-ought-to-be-spanked'; but I'm going to call her Taffy. And she was Tegumai Bopsulai's Best Beloved and her own Mummy's Best Beloved, and she was not spanked half as much as was good for her; and they were all three very happy. As soon as Taffy could run about she went everywhere with her Daddy Tegumai, and sometimes they would not come home to the Cave till they were hungry, and then Teshumai Tewindrow would say, 'Where in the world have you two been to, to get so shocking dirty? Really, my Tegumai, you're no better than my Taffy.'

Now attend and listen!

One day Tegumai Bopsulai went down through the beaver-swamp to the Wagai river to spear carp-fish for dinner, and Taffy went too. Tegumai's spear was made of wood with shark's teeth at the end, and before he had caught any fish at all he accidentally broke it clean across by jabbing it down too hard on the bottom of the river. They were miles and miles from home (of course they had their lunch with them in a little bag), and Tegumai had forgotten to bring any extra spears.

'Here's a pretty kettle of fish!' said Tegumai. 'It will take me half the day to mend this.'

'There's your big black spear at home,' said Taffy. 'Let me run back to the Cave and ask Mummy to give it me.'

'It's too far for your little fat legs,' said Tegumai. 'Besides, you might fall into the beaver-swamp and be drowned. We must make the best of a bad job.' He sat down and took out a little leather mendy-bag, full of reindeer-sinews and strips of leather, and lumps of bee's-wax and resin, and began to mend the spear. Taffy sat down too, with her toes in the water and her chin in her hand, and thought very hard. Then she said—

'I say, Daddy, it's an awful nuisance that you and I don't know how to write, isn't it? If we did we could send a message for the new spear.'

'Taffy,' said Tegumai, 'how often have I told you not to use slang? "Awful" isn't a pretty word,—but it *would* be a convenience, now you mention it, if we could write home.'

Just then a Stranger-man came along the river, but he belonged to a far tribe, the Tewaras, and he did not understand one word of Tegumai's language. He stood on the bank and smiled at Taffy, because he had a little girl-daughter of his own at home. Tegumai drew a hank of deer-sinews from his mendy-bag and began to mend his spear.

'Come here,' said Taffy. 'Do you know where my Mummy lives?' And the Stranger-man said 'Um!'—being, as you know, a Tewara.

'Silly!' said Taffy, and she stamped her foot, because she saw a shoal of very big carp going up the river just when her Daddy couldn't use his spear.

'Don't bother grown-ups,' said Tegumai, so busy with his spear-mending that he did not turn round.

'I aren't,' said Taffy. 'I only want him to do what I want him to do, and he won't understand.'

'Then don't bother me,' said Tegumai, and he went on pulling and straining at the deer-sinews with his mouth full of loose ends. The Stranger-man—a genuine Tewara he was—sat down on the grass, and Taffy showed him what her Daddy was doing. The Stranger-man thought, 'This is a very wonderful child. She stamps her foot at me and she makes faces. She must be the daughter of that noble Chief who is so great that he won't take any notice of me.' So he smiled more politely than ever.

'Now,' said Taffy, 'I want you to go to my Mummy, because your legs are longer than mine, and you won't fall into the beaver-swamp, and ask for Daddy's other spear—the one with the black handle that hangs over our fireplace.'

The Stranger-man (*and* he was a Tewara) thought, 'This is a very, very wonderful child. She waves her arms and she shouts at me, but I don't understand a word of what she says.

But if I don't do what she wants, I greatly fear that that haughty Chief, Man-who-turns-his-back-on-callers, will be angry.' He got up and twisted a big flat piece of bark off a birch-tree and gave it to Taffy. He did this, Best Beloved, to show that his heart was as white as the birch-bark and that he meant no harm; but Taffy didn't quite understand.

'Oh!' said she. 'Now I see! You want my Mummy's living-address? Of course I can't write, but I can draw pictures if I've anything sharp to scratch with. Please lend me the shark's tooth off your necklace.'

The Stranger-man (and *he* was a Tewara) didn't say anything, so Taffy put up her little hand and pulled at the beautiful bead and seed and shark-tooth necklace round his neck.

The Stranger-man (and he *was* a Tewara) thought, 'This is a very, very, very wonderful child. The shark's tooth on my necklace is a magic shark's tooth, and I was always told that if anybody touched it without my leave they would immediately swell up or burst. But this child doesn't swell up or burst, and that important Chief, Man-who-attends-strictly-to-his-business, who has not yet taken any notice of me at all, doesn't seem to be afraid that she will swell up or burst. I had better be more polite.'

So he gave Taffy the shark's tooth, and she lay down flat on her tummy with her legs in the air, like some people on the drawing-room floor when they want to draw pictures, and she said, 'Now I'll draw you some beautiful pictures! You can look over my shoulder, but you mustn't joggle. First I'll draw Daddy fishing. It isn't very like him; but Mummy will know, because I've drawn his spear all broken. Well, now I'll draw the other spear that he wants, the black-handled spear. It looks as if it was sticking in Daddy's back, but that's because the shark's tooth slipped and this piece of bark isn't big enough. That's the spear I want you to fetch; so I'll draw a picture of me myself 'splaining to you. My hair doesn't stand up like I've drawn, but it's easier to draw that way. Now I'll draw you. *I* think you're very nice really, but I can't make you pretty in the picture, so you mustn't be 'fended. Are you 'fended?'

The Stranger-man (and he was *a* Tewara) smiled. He thought, 'There must be a big battle going to be fought somewhere, and this extraordinary child, who takes my magic shark's tooth but who does not swell up or burst, is telling me to call all the great Chief's tribe to help him. He *is* a great Chief, or he would have noticed me.'

'Look,' said Taffy, drawing very hard and

'Now I'll draw you some beautiful pictures!
You can look over my shoulder, but you mustn't
joggle.'

rather scratchily, 'now I've drawn you, and I've put the spear that Daddy wants into your hand, just to remind you that you're to bring it. Now I'll show you how to find my Mummy's living-address. You go along till you come to two trees (those are trees), and then you go over a hill (that's a hill), and then you come into a beaver-swamp all full of beavers. I haven't put in all the beavers, because I can't draw beavers, but I've drawn their heads, and that's all you'll see of them when you cross the swamp. Mind you don't fall in! Then our Cave is just beyond the beaver-swamp. It isn't as high as the hills really, but I can't draw things very small. That's my Mummy outside. She is beautiful. She is the most beautifullest Mummy there ever was, but she won't be 'fended when she sees I've drawn her so plain. She'll be pleased of me because I can draw. Now, in case you forget, I've drawn the spear that Daddy wants *outside* our Cave. It's *inside* really, but you show the picture to my Mummy and she'll give it you. I've made her holding up her hands, because I know she'll be so pleased to see you. Isn't it a beautiful picture? And do you quite understand, or shall I 'splain again?'

The Stranger-man (and he was a *Tewara*) looked at the picture and nodded very hard. He said to himself, 'If I do not fetch this great

Chief's tribe to help him, he will be slain by his enemies who are coming up on all sides with spears. Now I see why the great Chief pretended not to notice me! He feared that his enemies were hiding in the bushes and would see him deliver a message to me. Therefore he turned his back, and let the wise and wonderful child draw the terrible picture showing me his difficulties. I will away and get help for him from his tribe.' He did not even ask Taffy the road, but raced off into the bushes like the wind, with the birch-bark in his hand, and Taffy sat down most pleased.

Now this is the picture that Taffy had drawn for him!

'What have you been doing, Taffy?' said Tegumai. He had mended his spear and was carefully waving it to and fro.

'It's a little berangement of my own, Daddy dear,' said Taffy. 'If you won't ask me questions, you'll know all about it in a little time, and you'll be surprised. You don't know how surprised you'll be, Daddy! Promise you'll be surprised.'

'Very well,' said Tegumai, and went on fishing.

The Stranger-man—did you know he was a Tewara?—hurried away with the picture and ran for some miles, till quite by accident he found Teshumai Tewindrow at the door of her Cave, talking to some other Neolithic ladies who had come in to a Primitive lunch. Taffy was very like Teshumai, specially about the upper part of the face and the eyes, so the Stranger-man—always a pure Tewara—smiled politely and handed Teshumai the birch-bark. He had run hard, so that he panted, and his legs were scratched with brambles, but he still tried to be polite.

As soon as Teshumai saw the picture she screamed like anything and flew at the Stranger-man. The older Neolithic ladies at once knocked him down and sat on him in a long line of six, while Teshumai pulled his hair. 'It's as plain as the nose on this Stranger-man's face,' she said. 'He has stuck my Tegu-mai all full of spears, and frightened poor Taffy so that her hair stands all on end; and not content with that, he brings me a horrid picture of how it was done. Look!' She showed the picture to all the Neolithic ladies sitting patiently on the Stranger-man. 'Here is my Tegumai with his arm broken; here is a spear sticking into his back; here is a man with a spear ready to throw; here is another man throwing a spear from a Cave, and here are a whole pack of people' (they were Taffy's beavers really, but they did look rather like people) 'coming up behind Tegumai. Isn't it shocking!'

'Most shocking!' said the Neolithic ladies, and they filled the Stranger-man's hair with mud (at which he was surprised), and they beat upon the Reverberating Tribal Drums, and called together all the chiefs of the Tribe of Tegumai, with their Hetmans and Dolmans, all Neguses, Woons, and Akhoonds of the organisation, in addition to the Warlocks, Angekoks, Juju-men, Bonzes, and the rest, who decided that before they chopped the Stranger-man's head off he should instantly lead them down to the river and show them where he had hidden poor Taffy.

By this time the Stranger-man (in spite of being a Tewara) was really annoyed. They had filled his hair quite solid with mud; they had rolled him up and down on knobby pebbles; they had sat upon him in a long line of six; they had thumped him and bumped him till he could hardly breathe; and though he did not understand their language, he was almost sure that the names the Neolithic ladies called him were not ladylike. However, he said nothing till all the Tribe of Tegumai were assembled, and then he led them back to the bank of the Wagai river, and there they found Taffy making daisy-chains, and Tegumai carefully spearing small carp with his mended spear.

'Well, you *have* been quick!' said Taffy. 'But why did you bring so many people? Daddy dear, this is my surprise. *Are* you surprised, Daddy?'

'Very,' said Tegumai; 'but it has ruined all my fishing for the day. Why, the whole dear, kind, nice, clean, quiet Tribe is here, Taffy.'

And so they were. First of all walked Teshu-mai Tewindrow and the Neolithic ladies, tightly holding on to the Stranger-man, whose hair was full of mud (although he was a Te-wara). Behind them came the Head Chief, the Vice-Chief, the Deputy and Assistant Chiefs (all armed to the upper teeth), the Hetmans and Heads of Hundreds, Platoffs with their Platoons, and Dolmans with their Detachments; Woons, Neguses, and Akhoonds ranking in the rear (still armed to the teeth). Behind them was the Tribe in hierarchical order, from owners of four caves (one for each season), a private reindeer-run, and two salmon-leaps, to feudal and prognathous Villeins, semi-entitled to half a bearskin of winter nights, seven yards from the fire, and adscript serfs, holding the reversion of a scraped marrow-bone under heriot (Aren't those beautiful words, Best Beloved?). They were all there, prancing and shouting, and they frightened every fish for twenty miles, and Tegumai thanked them in a fluid Neolithic oration.

Then Teshumai Tewindrow ran down and kissed and hugged Taffy very much indeed; but the Head Chief of the Tribe of Tegumai took Tegumai by the top-knot feathers and shook him severely.

'Explain! Explain! Explain!' cried all the Tribe of Tegumai.

'Goodness' sakes alive!' said Tegumai. 'Let go of my top-knot. Can't a man break his carp-spear without the whole countryside descending on him? You're a very interfering people.'

'I don't believe you've brought my Daddy's

black-handled spear after all,' said Taffy. 'And what *are* you doing to my nice Stranger-man?'

They were thumping him by twos and threes and tens till his eyes turned round and round. He could only gasp and point at Taffy.

'Where are the bad people who speared you, my darling?' said Teshumai Tewindrow.

'There weren't any,' said Tegumai. 'My only visitor this morning was the poor fellow that you are trying to choke. Aren't you well, or are you ill, O Tribe of Tegumai?'

'He came with a horrible picture,' said the Head Chief,—'a picture that showed you were full of spears.'

'Er—um—P'raps I'd better 'splain that I gave him that picture,' said Taffy, but she did not feel quite comfy.

'You!' said the Tribe of Tegumai all together. 'Small-person-with-no-manners-who-ought-to-be-spanked! You?'

'Taffy dear, I'm afraid we're in for a little trouble,' said her Daddy, and put his arm round her, so she didn't care.

'Explain! Explain! Explain!' said the Head Chief of the Tribe of Tegumai, and he hopped on one foot.

'I wanted the Stranger-man to fetch Daddy's spear, so I drawded it,' said Taffy. 'There wasn't lots of spears. There was only one spear. I drawded it three times to make sure. I couldn't help it looking as if it struck into Daddy's head—there wasn't room on the birch-bark; and those things that Mummy called bad people are my beavers. I drawded them to show him the way through the swamp; and I drawded Mummy at the mouth of the Cave looking pleased because he is a nice Stranger-man, and *I* think you are just the stupidest people in the world,' said Taffy. 'He is a very nice man. Why have you filled his hair with mud? Wash him!'

Nobody said anything at all for a long time, till the Head Chief laughed; then the Stranger-man (who was a least a Tewara) laughed; then Tegumai laughed till he fell down flat on the bank; then all the Tribe laughed more and worse and louder. The only people who did not laugh were Teshumai Tewindrow and all the Neolithic ladies. They were very polite to all their husbands, and said 'idiot!' ever so often.

Then the Head Chief of the Tribe of Tegumai cried and said and sang, 'O Small-person-without-any-manners-who-ought-to-be-spanked, you've hit upon a great invention!'

'I didn't intend to; I only wanted Daddy's black-handled spear,' said Taffy.

'Never mind. It *is* a great invention, and

some day men will call it writing. At present it is only pictures, and, as we have seen to-day, pictures are not always properly understood. But a time will come, O Babe of Tegumai, when we shall make letters—all twenty-six of 'em,—and when we shall be able to read as well as to write, and then we shall always say exactly what we mean without any mistakes. Let the Neolithic ladies wash the mud out of the stranger's hair!'

'I shall be glad of that,' said Taffy, 'because, after all, though you've brought every single other spear in the Tribe of Tegumai, you've forgotten my Daddy's black-handled spear.'

Then the Head Chief cried and said and sang, 'Taffy dear, the next time you write a picture-letter, you'd better send a man who can talk our language with it, to explain what it means. I don't mind it myself, because I am a Head Chief, but it's very bad for the rest of the Tribe of Tegumai, and, as you can see, it surprises the stranger.'

Then they adopted the Stranger-man (a genuine Tewara of Tewar) into the Tribe of Tegumai, because he was a gentleman and did not make a fuss about the mud that the Neolithic ladies had put into his hair. But from that day to this (and I suppose it is all Taffy's fault), very few little girls have ever liked learning to read or write. Most of them prefer to draw pictures and play about with their Daddies— just like Taffy.

THERE runs a road by Merrow Down—
    A grassy track to-day it is—
An hour out of Guildford town,
    Above the river Wey it is.

Here, when they heard the horse-bells ring,
    The ancient Britons dressed and rode
To watch the dark Phœnicians bring
    Their goods along the Western Road.

And here, or hereabouts, they met
    To hold their racial talks and such—
To barter beads for Whitby jet,
    And tin for gay shell torques and such.

But long and long before that time
    (When bison used to roam on it)
Did Taffy and her Daddy climb
    That down, and had their home on it.

Then beavers built in Broadstonebrook
    And made a swamp where Bramley stands;
And bears from Shere would come and look
    For Taffimai where Shamley stands.

The Wey, that Taffy called Wagai,
    Was more than six times bigger then;
And all the Tribe of Tegumai
    They cut a noble figure then!

How the Alphabet Was Made

THE WEEK AFTER Taffimai Metallumai (we will still call her Taffy, Best Beloved) made that little mistake about her Daddy's spear and the Stranger-man and the picture-letter and all, she went carp-fishing again with her Daddy. Her Mummy wanted her to stay at home and help hang up hides to dry on the big drying-poles outside their Neolithic Cave, but Taffy slipped away down to her Daddy quite early, and they fished. Presently she began to giggle, and her Daddy said, 'Don't be silly, child.'

'But wasn't it inciting!' said Taffy. 'Don't you remember how the Head Chief puffed out his cheeks, and how funny the nice Stranger-man looked with the mud in his hair?'

'Well do I,' said Tegumai. 'I had to pay two deerskins—soft ones with fringes—to the Stranger-man for the things we did to him.'

'*We* didn't do anything,' said Taffy. 'It was Mummy and the other Neolithic ladies—and the mud.'

'We won't talk about that,' said her Daddy. 'Let's have lunch.'

Taffy took a marrow-bone and sat mousy-quiet for ten whole minutes, while her Daddy scratched on pieces of birch-bark with a shark's tooth. Then she said, 'Daddy, I've thinked of a secret surprise. You make a noise—any sort of noise.'

'Ah!' said Tegumai. 'Will that do to begin with?'

'Yes,' said Taffy. 'You look just like a carp-fish with its mouth open. Say it again, please.'

'Ah! ah! ah!' said her Daddy. 'Don't be rude, my daughter.'

'I'm not meaning rude, really and truly,' said Taffy. 'It's part of my secret-surprise-think. *Do* say *ah*, Daddy, and keep your mouth open at the end, and lend me that tooth. I'm going to draw a carp-fish's mouth wide-open.'

'What for?' said her Daddy.

'Don't you see?' said Taffy, scratching away on the bark. 'That will be our little secret s'prise. When I draw a carp-fish with his mouth open in the smoke at the back of our Cave—if Mummy doesn't mind—it will remind you of that ah-noise. Then we can play that it was me jumped out of the dark and s'prised you with that noise—same as I did in the beaver-swamp last winter.'

'Really?' said her Daddy, in the voice that grown-ups use when they are truly attending. 'Go on, Taffy.'

'Oh bother!' she said. 'I can't draw all of a carp-fish, but I can draw something that means a carp-fish's mouth. Don't you know how they stand on their heads rooting in the mud? Well, here's a pretence carp-fish (we can play that the rest of him is drawn). Here's just his mouth, and that means *ah*.' And she drew this. (1.)

'That's not bad,' said Tegumai, and scratched on his own piece of bark for himself; 'but you've forgotten the feeler that hangs across his mouth.'

'But I can't draw, Daddy.'

'You needn't draw anything of him except just the opening of his mouth and the feeler across. Then we'll know he's a carp-fish, 'cause the perches and trouts haven't got feelers. Look here, Taffy.' And he drew this. (2.)

'Now I'll copy it,' said Taffy. 'Will you understand *this* when you see it?' And
she drew this. (3.)

'Perfectly,' said her Daddy. 'And
I'll be quite as s'prised when I see
it anywhere, as if you had jumped
out from behind a tree and said "Ah!" '

3

'Now, make another noise,' said Taffy, very
proud.

'Yah!' said her Daddy, very loud.

'H'm,' said Taffy. 'That's a mixy noise. The
end part is *ah*-carp-fish-mouth; but what can
we do about the front part? *Yer-yer-yer* and
ah! Ya!'

'It's very like the carp-fish-mouth noise.
Let's draw another bit of the carp-fish and
join 'em,' said her Daddy. *He* was quite incited
too.

'No. If they're joined, I'll forget. Draw it sep-
arate. Draw his tail. If he's standing on his
head the tail will come first. 'Sides, I think I
can draw tails easiest,' said Taffy.

'A good notion,' said Tegumai. 'Here's a
carp-fish tail for the *yer*-noise.' And
he drew this. (4.)

'I'll try now,' said Taffy. "Member
I can't draw like you, Daddy. Will it
do if I just draw the split part of
the tail, and a sticky-down line for where

4

it joins?' And she drew this. (5.)

Her Daddy nodded, and his eyes were shiny bright with 'citement.

'That's beautiful,' she said. 'Now, make another noise, Daddy.'

'Oh!' said her Daddy, very loud.

'That's quite easy,' said Taffy. 'You make your mouth all round like an egg or a stone. So an egg or a stone will do for that.'

'You can't always find eggs or stones. We'll have to scratch a round something like one.' And he drew this. (6.)

'My gracious!' said Taffy, 'what a lot of noise-pictures we've made,— carp-mouth, carp-tail, and egg! Now, make another noise, Daddy.'

'Ssh!' said her Daddy, and frowned to himself, but Taffy was too incited to notice.

'That's quite easy,' she said, scratching on the bark.'

'Eh, what?' said her Daddy. 'I meant I was thinking, and didn't want to be disturbed.'

'It's a noise, just the same. It's the noise a snake makes, Daddy, when it is thinking and doesn't want to be disturbed. Let's make the *ssh*-noise a snake. Will this do?' And she drew this. (7.)

'There,' she said. 'That's another s'prise-secret. When you draw a

7

hissy-snake by the door of your little back-cave where you mend the spears, I'll know you're thinking hard; and I'll come in most mousy-quiet. And if you draw it on a tree by the river when you're fishing, I'll know you want me to walk most *most* mousy-quiet, so as not to shake the banks.'

'Perfectly true,' said Tegumai. 'And there's more in this game than you think. Taffy, dear, I've a notion that your Daddy's daughter has hit upon the finest thing that there ever was since the Tribe of Tegumai took to using shark's teeth instead of flints for their spear-heads. I believe we've found out *the* big secret of the world.'

'Why?' said Taffy, and her eyes shone too with incitement.

'I'll show,' said her Daddy. 'What's water in the Tegumai language?'

'*Ya*, of course, and it means river too—like Wagai-*ya*—the Wagai river.'

'What is bad water that gives you fever if you drink it—black water—swamp-water?'

'*Yo*, of course.'

'Now look,' said her Daddy. 'S'pose you saw this scratched by the side of a pool in the beaver-swamp?' And he drew this. (8.)

'Carp-tail and round egg. Two noises mixed! *Yo*, bad water,' said Taffy. ' 'Course I wouldn't drink that

8

water because I'd know you said it was bad.'

'But I needn't be near the water at all. I might be miles away, hunting, and still——'

'And *still* it would be just the same as if you stood there and said, "G'way, Taffy, or you'll get fever." All that in a carp-fish tail and a round egg! O Daddy, we must tell Mummy, quick!' and Taffy danced all round him.

'Not yet,' said Tegumai; 'not till we've gone a little further. Let's see. *Yo* is bad water, but *so* is food cooked on the fire, isn't it?' And he drew this. (9.)

'Yes. Snake and egg,' said Taffy. 'So that means dinner's ready. If you saw that scratched on a tree you'd know it was time to come to the Cave. So'd I.'

'My Winkie!' said Tegumai. 'That's true too. But wait a minute. I see a difficulty. *So* means "come and have dinner," but *sho* means the drying-poles where we hang our hides.'

'Horrid old drying-poles!' said Taffy. 'I hate helping to hang heavy, hot, hairy hides on them. If you drew the snake and egg, and I thought it meant dinner, and I came in from the wood and found that it meant I was to help Mummy hang the hides on the drying-poles, what *would* I do?'

'You'd be cross. So'd Mummy. We must make a new picture for *sho*. We must draw a spotty snake that hisses *sh-sh*, and we'll play that the plain snake only hisses *ssss*.'

'I couldn't be sure how to put in the spots,' said Taffy. 'And p'raps if *you* were in a hurry you might leave them out, and I'd think it was *so* when it was *sho*, and then Mummy would catch me just the same. *No!* I think we'd better draw a picture of the horrid high drying-poles their very selves, and make *quite* sure. I'll put 'em in just after the hissy-snake. Look!' And she drew this. (10.)

'P'raps that's safest. It's very like our drying-poles, anyhow,' said her Daddy, laughing. 'Now I'll make a new noise with a snake and drying-pole sound in it. I'll say *shi*. That's Tegumai for spear, Taffy.' And he laughed.

'Don't make fun of me,' said Taffy, as she thought of her picture-letter and the mud in the Stranger-man's hair. '*You* draw it, Daddy.'

'We won't have beavers or hills this time, eh?' said her Daddy. 'I'll just draw a straight line for my spear.' And he drew this. (11.)

'Even Mummy couldn't mistake that for me being killed.'

'*Please* don't, Daddy. It makes me uncomfy. Do some more noises. We're getting on beautifully.'

'Er-hm!' said Tegumai, looking up. 'We'll say *shu*. That means sky.'

Taffy drew the snake and the drying-pole. Then she stopped. 'We must make a new picture for that end sound, mustn't we?'

'*Shu-shu-u-u-u!*' said her Daddy. 'Why, it's just like the round-egg-sound made thin.'

'Then s'pose we draw a thin round egg, and pretend it's a frog that hasn't eaten anything for years.'

'N-no,' said her Daddy. 'If we drew that in a hurry we might mistake it for the round egg itself. *Shu-shu-shu! I'll* tell you what we'll do. We'll open a little hole at the end of the round egg to show how the O-noise runs out all thin, *ooo-oo-oo*. Like this.' And he drew this. (12.)

12

'Oh, that's lovely! Much better than a thin frog. Go on,' said Taffy, using her shark's tooth.

Her Daddy went on drawing, and his hand shook with incitement. He went on till he had drawn this. (13.)

'Don't look up, Taffy,' he said. 'Try if you can make out what that means in the Tegumai language. If you can, we've found the Secret.'

'Snake—pole—broken-egg—carp-tail   and

carp-mouth,' said Taffy. '*Shu-ya*. Sky-water (rain).' Just then a drop fell on her hand, for the day had clouded over. 'Why, Daddy, it's raining. Was *that* what you meant to tell me?'

'Of course,' said her Daddy. 'And I told it you without saying a word, didn't I?'

'Well, I *think* I would have known it in a minute, but that raindrop made me quite sure. I'll always remember now. *Shu-ya* means rain, or "it is going to rain." Why, Daddy!' She got up and danced round him. 'S'pose you went out before I was awake, and drawed *shu-ya* in the smoke on the wall, I'd know it was going to rain and I'd take my beaver-skin hood. Wouldn't Mummy be surprised!'

Tegumai got up and danced. (Daddies didn't mind doing those things in those days.) 'More than that! More than that!' he said. 'S'pose I wanted to tell you it wasn't going to rain much and you must come down to the river, what would we draw? Say the words in Tegumai-talk first.'

'*Shu-ya-las, ya maru.* (Sky-water ending. River come to.) *What* a lot of new sounds! *I* don't see how we can draw them.'

'But I do—but I do!' said Tegumai. 'Just attend a minute, Taffy, and we won't do any more to-day. We've got *shu-ya* all right, haven't we? but this *las* is a teaser. *La-la-la!*' and he waved his shark-tooth.

'There's the hissy-snake at the end and the carp-mouth before the snake—*as-as-as*. We only want *la-la*,' said Taffy.

'I know it, but we have to make *la-la*. And we're the first people in all the world who've ever tried to do it, Taffimai!'

'Well,' said Taffy, yawning, for she was rather tired. '*Las* means breaking or finishing as well as ending, doesn't it?'

'So it does,' said Tegumai. '*Ya-las* means that there's no water in the tank for Mummy to cook with—just when I'm going hunting, too.'

'And *shi-las* means that your spear is broken. If I'd only thought of *that* instead of drawing silly beaver-pictures for the Stranger!'

'*La! La! La!*' said Tegumai, waving his stick and frowning. 'Oh bother!'

'I could have drawn *shi* quite easily,' Taffy went on. 'Then I'd have drawn your spear all broken—this way!' And she drew. (14.)

'The very thing,' said Tegumai. 'That's

14

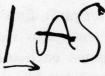

15

16

la all over. It isn't like any of the other marks,
either.' And he drew this. (15.)

'Now for *ya*. Oh, we've done that before.
Now for *maru*. *Mum-mum-mum*. *Mum* shuts
one's mouth up, doesn't it? We'll draw a shut
mouth like this.' And he drew. (16.)

'Then the carp-mouth open. That makes
Ma-ma-ma! But what about this *rrrrr*-thing,
Taffy?'

'It sounds all rough and edgy, like your
shark-tooth saw when you're cutting out a
plank for the canoe,' said Taffy.

'You mean all sharp at the
edges, like this?' said Tegumai.
And he drew. (17.)

17

''Xactly,' said Taffy. 'But we
don't want all those teeth: only put two.'

'I'll only put in one,' said Tegumai. 'If this
game of ours is going to be what I think it
will, the easier we make our
sound-pictures the better for everybody.' And he drew. (18.)

'*Now* we've got it,' said Tegumai,
standing on one leg. 'I'll draw 'em
all in a string like fish.'

18

'Hadn't we better put a little bit of stick or
something between each word, so's they
won't rub up against each other and jostle,
same as if they were carps?'

'Oh, I'll leave a space for that,' said her Daddy. And very incitedly he drew them all without stopping, on a big new bit of birch-bark. (19.)

'*Shu-ya-las ya-maru,*' said Taffy, reading it out sound by sound.

19

'That's enough for to-day,' said Tegumai. 'Besides, you're getting tired, Taffy. Never mind, dear. We'll finish it all to-morrow, and then we'll be remembered for years and years after the biggest trees you can see are all chopped up for firewood.'

So they went home, and all that evening Tegumai sat on one side of the fire and Taffy on the other, drawing *ya's* and *yo's* and *shu's* and *shi's* in the smoke on the wall and gig-gling together till her Mummy said, 'Really, Tegumai, you're worse than my Taffy.'

'Please don't mind,' said Taffy. 'It's only our secret-s'prise, Mummy dear, and we'll tell you all about it the very minute it's done; but *please* don't ask me what it is now, or else I'll have to tell.'

So her Mummy most carefully didn't; and

bright and early next morning Tegumai went down to the river to think about new sound-pictures, and when Taffy got up she saw *Yalas* (water is ending or running out) chalked on the side of the big stone water-tank, outside the Cave.

'Um,' said Taffy. 'These picture-sounds are rather a bother! Daddy's just as good as come here himself and told me to get more water for Mummy to cook with.' She went to the spring at the back of the house and filled the tank from a bark bucket, and then she ran down to the river and pulled her Daddy's left ear—the one that belonged to her to pull when she was good.

'Now come along and we'll draw all the left-over sound-pictures,' said her Daddy, and they had a most inciting day of it, and a beautiful lunch in the middle, and two games of romps. When they came to T, Taffy said that as her name, and her Daddy's, and her Mummy's all began with that sound, they should draw a sort of family group of themselves holding hands. That was all very well to draw once or twice; but when it came to drawing it six or seven times, Taffy and Tegumai drew it scratchier and scratchier, till at last the T-sound was only a thin long Tegumai with his arms out to hold Taffy and Teshumai. You can

'Um,' said Taffy. 'These picture-sounds are rather a bother!'

see from these three pictures partly how it
happened. (20, 21, 22.)

Many of the other pictures were much too
beautiful to begin with, especially before
lunch; but as they were drawn over and over

20   21   22   23

again on birch-bark, they became plainer and
easier, till at last even Tegumai said he could
find no fault with them. They turned the hissy-
snake the other way round for the Z-sound, to
show it was hissing backwards in a soft and

24   25   26   27

gentle way (23); and they just made a twiddle
for E, because it came into the pictures so
often (24); and they drew pictures of the
sacred Beaver of the Tegumais for the B-
sound (25, 26, 27, 28); and because it was a
nasty, nosy noise, they just drew noses for the
N-sound, till they were tired (29); and they
drew a picture of the big lake-pike's mouth
for the greedy Ga-sound (30); and they drew

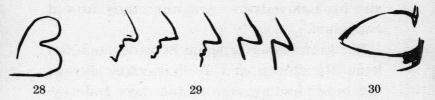

28   29   30

the pike's mouth again with a spear behind it
for the scratchy, hurty Ka-sound (31); and
they drew pictures of a little bit of the wind-
ing Wagai river for the nice windy-windy Wa-
sound (32, 33); and so on and so forth and so
following till they had done and drawn all the

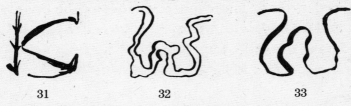

31   32   33

sound-pictures that they wanted, and there
was the Alphabet, all complete.

And after thousands and thousands and
thousands of years, and after Hieroglyphics,
and Demotics, and Nilotics, and Cryptics, and
Cufics, and Runics, and Dorics, and Ionics,
and all sorts of other ricks and tricks
(because the Woons, and the Neguses, and the
Akhoonds, and the Repositories of Tradition
would never leave a good thing alone when
they saw it), the fine old easy, understandable
Alphabet—A, B, C, D, E, and the rest of 'em—
got back into its proper shape again for

all Best Beloveds to learn when they are old enough.

But *I* remember Tegumai Bopsulai, and Taffimai Metallumai and Teshumai Tewindrow, her dear Mummy, and all the days gone by. And it was so—just so—a long time ago—on the banks of the big Wagai!

Of all the Tribe of Tegumai
   Who cut that figure, none remain,—
On Merrow Down the cuckoos cry—
   The silence and the sun remain.

But as the faithful years return
   And hearts unwounded sing again,
Comes Taffy dancing through the fern
   To lead the Surrey spring again.

Her brows are bound with bracken-fronds,
   And golden elf-locks fly above;
Her eyes are bright as diamonds
   And bluer than the skies above.

In moccasins and deer-skin cloak,
   Unfearing, free and fair she flits,
And lights her little damp-wood smoke
   To show her Daddy where she flits.

For far—oh, very far behind,
   So far she cannot call to him,
Comes Tegumai alone to find
   The daughter that was all to him.

CHILDREN'S THRIFT CLASSICS

Just $1.00
All books complete and unabridged, except where noted.
96pp., 5³/₁₆″ × 8¼″, paperbound.

AESOP'S FABLES, Aesop. 28020-9

THE LITTLE MERMAID AND OTHER FAIRY TALES, Hans Christian Andersen. 27816-6

THE UGLY DUCKLING AND OTHER FAIRY TALES, Hans Christian Andersen. 27081-5

THE THREE BILLY GOATS GRUFF AND OTHER READ-ALOUD STORIES, Carolyn Sherwin Bailey (ed.). 28021-7

THE STORY OF PETER PAN, James M. Barrie and Daniel O'Connor. 27294-X

ROBIN HOOD, Bob Blaisdell. 27573-6

THE ADVENTURES OF BUSTER BEAR, Thornton W. Burgess. 27564-7

THE ADVENTURES OF CHATTERER THE RED SQUIRREL, Thornton W. Burgess. 27399-7

THE ADVENTURES OF DANNY MEADOW MOUSE, Thornton W. Burgess. 27565-5

THE ADVENTURES OF GRANDFATHER FROG, Thornton W. Burgess. 27400-4

THE ADVENTURES OF JERRY MUSKRAT, Thornton W. Burgess. 27817-4

THE ADVENTURES OF JIMMY SKUNK, Thornton W. Burgess. 28023-3

THE ADVENTURES OF PETER COTTONTAIL, Thornton W. Burgess. 26929-9

THE ADVENTURES OF POOR MRS. QUACK, Thornton W. Burgess. 27818-2

THE ADVENTURES OF REDDY FOX, Thornton W. Burgess. 26930-2

THE SECRET GARDEN, Frances Hodgson Burnett. (abridged) 28024-1

PICTURE FOLK-TALES, Valery Carrick. 27083-1

THE STORY OF POCAHONTAS, Brian Doherty (ed.). 28025-X

SLEEPING BEAUTY AND OTHER FAIRY TALES, Jacob and Wilhelm Grimm. 27084-X

THE ELEPHANT'S CHILD AND OTHER JUST SO STORIES, Rudyard Kipling. 27821-2

HOW THE LEOPARD GOT HIS SPOTS AND OTHER JUST SO STORIES, Rudyard Kipling. 27297-4

MOWGLI STORIES FROM "THE JUNGLE BOOK," Rudyard Kipling. 28030-6

NONSENSE POEMS, Edward Lear. 28031-4

BEAUTY AND THE BEAST AND OTHER FAIRY TALES, Marie Leprince de Beaumont and Charles Perrault. 28032-2

A DOG OF FLANDERS, Ouida (Marie Louise de la Ramée). 27087-4

PETER RABBIT AND 11 OTHER FAVORITE TALES, Beatrix Potter. 27845-X

CHILDREN'S THRIFT CLASSICS

Just $1.00

All books complete and unabridged, except where noted.
96pp., 5³/₁₆″ × 8¼″, paperbound.

BLACK BEAUTY, Anna Sewell. (abridged) 27570-1

ALADDIN AND OTHER FAVORITE ARABIAN NIGHTS STORIES, Philip Smith (ed.). 27571-X

FAVORITE NORTH AMERICAN INDIAN LEGENDS, Philip Smith (ed.). 27822-0

FAVORITE POEMS OF CHILDHOOD, Philip Smith (ed.). 27089-0

IRISH FAIRY TALES, Philip Smith (ed.). 27572-8 $1.00

JAPANESE FAIRY TALES, Philip Smith (ed.). 27300-8

A CHILD'S GARDEN OF VERSES, Robert Louis Stevenson. 27301-6

THE HAPPY PRINCE AND OTHER FAIRY TALES, Oscar Wilde. 27091-2

Write for a free full-color Juvenile Book Catalog (59071-2).